Gilbert
de la frogponde

— a swamp story —

written by jennifer rae

illustrated by rose cowles

PEACHTREE
ATLANTA

Published by
PEACHTREE PUBLISHERS, LTD.
494 Armour Circle NE
Atlanta, Georgia 30324

Text © 1997 by Jennifer Rae
Illustrations © 1997 by Rose Cowles
First published by Whitecap Books Ltd., Canada, 1997.
First United States edition published by Peachtree Publishers, Ltd., 1997.

Book design and composition by Rose Cowles

Printed in Hong Kong

10 9 8 7 6 5 4 3 2 1
First Edition

Library of Congress Cataloging-in-Publication Data

Rae, Jennifer
      Gilbert de la Frogponde / written by Jennifer Rae ; illustrated by
Rose Cowles.
         p. cm.
      Summary: A clever, plump frog convinces two gourmet chefs that
bugs, not frogs, are all the rage in the chicest culinary circles.
      ISBN 1-56145-163-0
      [1. Frogs—Fiction. 2. Stories in rhyme.] I. Cowles, Rose, ill.
II. Title.
PZ8.3.R1185Gi 1997
[E]—dc21
                                           97-19638
                                               CIP
                                               AC

Gilbert was a hopper
with an appetite for bugs—
for caterpillars, dragonflies,
and juicy little slugs.

He ate so many winged things
for oh so many moons
that he blew up (when he grew up)
to the size of a balloon.

Since Gilbert
was **enormous,**

but because his feet were small,

the hefty little hopper

couldn't swim a stroke at all.

So while his friends went swimming

in their frankly froglike ways,

he flopped upon deserted docks

and **slept away the days.**

One day the calm was broken

when a pair of gourmet cooks

came hunting 'round the frog pond

for some frogs to bait their hooks.

And they heaped a pile of slugs and flies

up high upon a dish

to tempt the little hoppers,

who would surely tempt the fish.

The hoppers heard the ruckus
and they scurried out of sight.
They hid beneath the water
where they shook with froglike **fright**.

And all across the frog pond
from the rowboat to the shore,
not a sound or splash was heard
except a **single, soggy snore.**

The cooks looked 'round in wonder.

They rubbed their eyes in **shock**.

The one said to the other,

"Do you see what's on the dock?"

"A frog so slow and sleepy
and so big and meaty, too.
Why bother catching small frogs?
We can **cut** this one in two!"

That got the cooks to thinking
and the first one scratched his head:

"What need have we
for fish at all?
Let's eat this
frog instead."

"We'll have his arms for supper
and his chubby legs for lunch.
The rest of him we'll squeeze
into a sausage
for our brunch!"

Poor Gilbert heard them scheming.

Poor Gilbert saw his fate.

He closed his eyes and visualized

his legs upon a plate.

And so to save his slimy skin

he cleared his croaky throat,

and spinning on his frog's legs • • •

"My friends,
you must be gourmet chefs,
and so am I, you see.
I'm Gilbert de la Frogponde—
that's la Frogponde
with an **'e.'**"

"And I'll share with you a secret,
as I see you've got some slugs.
Frogs are très passé these days—
the latest thing is

bugs!"

"Oh yes,
there's Hornet Jalapeño,
there's Caterpillar Stew,

and Horsefly
Primavera,

though the wings are hard to chew."

"Centipede Salade's divine
for something fresh and light.
But watch out
for Mosquito Quiche—
I itched
and scratched
all night!"

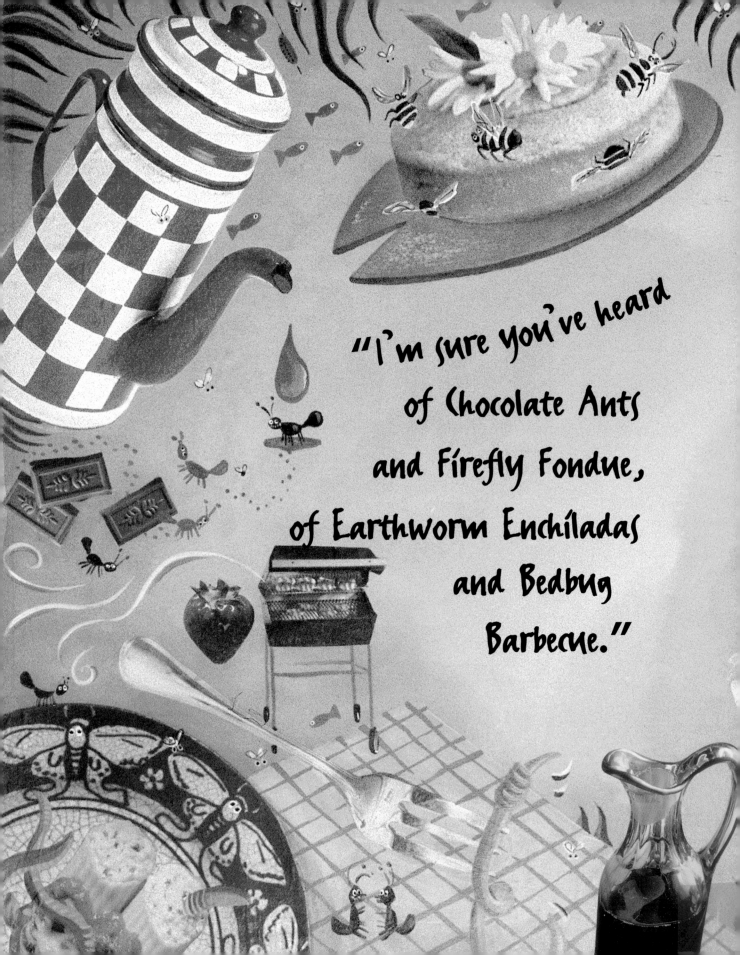

"I'm sure you've heard of Chocolate Ants and Firefly Fondue, of Earthworm Enchiladas and Bedbug Barbecue."

The chefs looked at the frog and asked:

"What is this new cuisine?
The flavors sound exotic,
though the portions seem quite lean."
"But if eating bugs is all the rage
I guess we probably should..."

They gobbled up some slugs and cried,

"They're really rather good!"

The chefs threw down their fishpoles
and scrambled to the shore.

"We need those recipes!" they cried.

"You've got to tell us more!"

So they talked and **ate** for hours,

till they'd finished

all the **slugs.**

Then they all fell

fast

asleep . . .